CHEETAH LEARNS TO PLAY NICELY

A book about being a GOOD SPORT

Written by Sue Graves

Illustrated by Trevor Dunton

W

FRANKLIN WATTS
LONDON • SYDNEY

Cheetah loved playing sport. Best of all, he loved to win. But Cheetah did not play nicely. He was **not a good sport at all**!

When his team lost at football, he **shook his fists** and **sulked**.

When he didn't win at swimming, he threw his towel into the pool. Everyone was cross with Cheetah for being **a bad sport**.

But Cheetah said he didn't care. He said he just wanted to be the best and to **win everything**.

One day Mr Croc took everyone to Fun Jungle. Everyone was **very excited**. There were nets to scramble under, zip wires to zoom along and swamps to wade through.

At Fun Jungle, Mr Croc got out his big
stopwatch to see who was the fastest
to get round. He said the record for the
fastest time was 15 minutes.

Cheetah **boasted** that he would win and
that he would beat the record **easily**.
Hippo was cross. He said it was better
to **try hard** and to be a **good sport**.

Then Mr Croc blew his whistle and everyone ran.
Cheetah ran off as fast as he could.

He scrambled under the net easily... but he **did not stop** to help Giraffe who got stuck. Giraffe said Cheetah was a **bad sport** not to help.

Then it was the zip wire. Mr Croc said they had to **take turns**. Hippo went first, but he fell off and had to start all over again. Cheetah got cross. He said he wanted **his turn now**! Hippo said Cheetah was a bad sport not to wait patiently.

13

After the zip wire it was the swamp.
It was very deep. Cheetah waded through it
easily... but he didn't stop to help Monkey
who had fallen in.

Monkey was upset. He said Cheetah was
a bad sport not to help him.

But Cheetah took no notice.

Cheetah got to the finishing line and ran across it as fast as he could. He boasted that he had beaten the record **easily**.

Mr Croc checked his stopwatch. He said Cheetah had done well but he hadn't beaten the record. Cheetah was cross. He **stamped his feet** and he **sulked**.

Cheetah wanted to try again to beat the record.
He asked his friends to go with him. But his friends
said **no**, and that he was a **bad sport**.
They said he would have to go round **on his own**.

Cheetah was sad. He didn't mean to upset his friends. And he didn't want to go round Fun Jungle on his own. That would be **no fun at all**!

Cheetah went to see Mr Croc. He told him that he had been a bad sport. He told him that his friends were cross with him. Mr Croc asked him what he should do to **put things right**.

Cheetah had a think. He said he should
say sorry to his friends for being such a bad
sport. He said he should **play nicely** in future.
Mr Croc said these were good ideas.

Cheetah said sorry to his friends. He said he would try hard to be a **good sport** in future. He said he would try hard to **play nicely**.

Everyone agreed to go round Fun Jungle again
so long as Cheetah promised to be a good sport.
Cheetah **promised**.

This time, Cheetah helped Giraffe under the net. Giraffe didn't **get stuck**.

Cheetah steadied the zip wire for Hippo. Hippo didn't **fall off**.

24

Best of all, Cheetah helped Monkey through the swamp. Monkey didn't **fall in**.

They all ran to the finishing line.
Cheetah ran fast but he didn't break the record.
Cheetah **did not mind at all**. He said it was
more fun to play nicely and to be a good sport.
Everyone agreed!

A note about sharing this book

The *Behaviour Matters* series has been developed to provide a starting point for further discussion on children's behaviour both in relation to themselves and others. The series is set in the jungle with animal characters reflecting typical behaviour traits often seen in young children.

Cheetah Learns to Play Nicely
This story looks at the importance of playing fairly and of being a good sport. It aims to encourage children to enjoy sport but not to be so intent on winning that they spoil others' games.

How to use the book
The book is designed for adults to share with either an individual child, or a group of children, and as a starting point for discussion.

The book also provides visual support and repeated words and phrases to build reading confidence.

Before reading the story
Choose a time to read when you and the children are relaxed and have time to share the story.

Spend time looking at the illustrations and talk about what the book might be about before reading it together.

Encourage children to employ a phonics first approach to tackling new words by sounding the words out.

After reading, talk about the book with the children:

- Talk about the story with the children. Encourage them to retell the events in chronological order.

- Talk about Cheetah's behaviour. Was he unkind not to help the other animals when they got into difficulties?

- Ask the children to explain how they feel when they are playing games or taking part in sport. Do they feel they have to win at all costs? Take the opportunity to point out that while winning is fun, it's better to play games fairly and to enjoy the experience of taking part.

- Why do the children think it is important that Cheetah apologises for his behaviour? Why might the other animals have resented his earlier behaviour? How would the children feel if someone like Cheetah spoiled their games and sports?

- Place the children into groups of three or four. Ask them to discuss the best way of playing games and sports with others and the behaviour that they would expect from them.

- Invite the groups to return and ask a spokesperson from each group to talk about their findings. Encourage the others to comment on these. Ask them to help you draw up a set of rules about how they should play games fairly and sportingly.

For Isabelle, William A, William G, George, Max, Emily, Leo, Caspar, Felix, Tabitha, Phoebe and Harry – S.G.

First published in Great Britain in 2018
by The Watts Publishing Group

Text © The Watts Publishing Group 2018
Illustrations © Trevor Dunton 2018

Series Editor: Jackie Hamley
Series Designer: Cathryn Gilbert

A CIP catalogue record for this book is
available from the British Library.

ISBN 978 1 4451 6979 8 (paperback)

Printed in China

Franklin Watts
An imprint of
Hachette Children's Group
Part of The Watts Publishing Group
Carmelite House
50 Victoria Embankment
London EC4Y 0DZ

Hachette Ireland
8 Castlecourt
Castleknock
Dublin 15
Ireland

An Hachette UK Company
www.hachette.co.uk

www.franklinwatts.co.uk

FSC
www.fsc.org
MIX
Paper from
responsible sources
FSC® C104740